BENJAMIN
AND
ISABELLA
GO GALLANTLY

A Novella by Rachelle Robinett

BENJAMIN
AND
ISABELLA
GO GALLANTLY

Based on a true story.

They met on a Monday. It was a warm day when cellophane leaves rustled on trees that wore them lazily. The canopy hung high like the surface of a chartreuse sea above which pulsed the sun, and the rest of the world. Below, the current was an unthreatening and wandering wind. Like her, it meandered the college avenues aimlessly indulging in small, swirling pleasures. Gusts scurried ahead of her shoes on the sidewalk chasing a confetti of litter and exploring edges. She floated on it, weightless without responsibility and lethargic with the relaxation that permeates deepest in midsummer.

A gentle, compulsive swell billowed at the small of her back and steered her into the café. Once inside, it slipped from her waist and dissolved into a sunny reflection on the dark wood floor. She stood amid a splayed fan of light before a room of mismatched tables and skewed chairs, unusually empty and all aglow. Rubbed-round corners bent sunlight sideways, quiet music fell from above and he stood alone behind the counter.

That day, the cafe felt like hers. Later, he told her that it had felt like his.

He straightened his shoulders and watched her approach. She'd seen him so many times before yet had never learned his name, and nor had he learned hers. Allowing no one to know her allowed any day to be different. This one was – it was hotter and slower and happier. So too she imagined it as her last in the city. She would talk about herself now that she wouldn't be back. She would let him in now that he couldn't stay. She would allow him to know her now that he could only know her as she was today. She'd like to learn something about him too. For fun, she would let down a guard and try her hand at small talk. It would be practice for the future – for when she arrived where she belonged and was surrounded by the people that she would want to know.

In keeping with the day's pace, she ordered tea rather than her usual Americano and they began chatting. *Are you enjoying the summer? Any plans for the weekend? What do you do? Yes, yes, etc. etc.*

While they talked, he turned and took a jar of faded leaves down from a top shelf. His forearms were tanned and strong. Muscles flickered beneath soft blonded hairs as he spooned the tea into an ivory linen bag and dropped it into a white paper cup. She smiled at the palette of the season. He had good posture. His back was shaped like an inverted triangle – shoulders widest and waist narrow where the apron was tied. She imagined him tying it before his shift, and then, untying it after. When he turned around, she was looking out the window.

She felt drunk enjoying the leisure – like a sigh and a stretch.

The tea steeped on the counter behind him. Purple and green crept through the cloth as a watercolor stain, blossoming into submerged thunderheads. She knew this because she usually watched it alone at her secluded table. Now though he remained between her and the billows, holding her in place while they grew.

His remarks were quick and smart. The conversation was coming effortlessly. She eased into eye contact, which seemed to have been his goal. They bantered about the question: "What do you do" and decided that it would be better to ask, "What is your passion?" as that is how we might actually be defined. She partook of his light green eyes and promking grin but she trusted that he smiled (like that) at all of the customers so she smirked at the counter top.

When the tea was ready, he passed it across the counter to her along with a CD.

He said, "This is what I do." He winked. "This is my passion. I make music."

She said, "Thank you."

"You're welcome."

Everything was so intentional.

A breeze blew open the door and they both looked to see no one enter. Her wind leapt up from the floor and bound out, pulling her with it. She resisted for a second to turn back and say goodbye. He was leaning on the counter, watching her leave and he nodded.

T hat afternoon, while driving somewhere, she listened to his music. She tore off the plastic and felt the smooth of the thick, paper cover. Prepared to be introduced, she slid the disc into the car stereo.

The first song started low. A piano chord. Silence. A chord, reverberation, silence. She held her breath. A trumpet. Chords, beats, a voice, female, nearly synthetic. The trumpet again, oh what a trumpet. Piercing, slow and long – stabbing like a lightweight's last jabs and then blown out to the end of breath, lingering, wavering, and finally swallowed by a swelling melody. The girl's voice pushed out on a new wave of sound, arriving like a gift in crisp glittering wrap that undid itself before her eyes. Notes tumbled in over each other through the speakers, lapping at her chest. She straightened and smiled. She saw sweat and shadows – the neon shoulders of a writhing club.

Grinning at a speaker she wondered, "Who have I met?"

The next song circled up around her, saturating the air in the car. It changed the colors of the view through the windshield like a curtain over the sun. Something between her ribs fluttered, caught and what she inhaled thickened. Perfume she could almost smell. Thrill. It was a temperature just past perception. A shiver. This was how music was supposed to feel. He knew what he was doing. It was bigger than she could consume all at once – attacking her from every direction though gently, aware of its effect. She sat very still and felt afloat.

(Here the background blurs a bit.)

She saw a slow pan across a barren landscape. The frame revealed and grew and then disappeared objects like holograms. Colored light displays like slow-motion fireworks exploded in the sky, their sparks showering onto a dry, black wasteland that stretched between her and a shimmering outline of structures on the horizon. Silhouettes were highlighted by the electric, ghost-city glow. She looked for the source of the serenade but the woman was always in the wings – her song an elusive, flitting shadow.

The album cover was black with charred orange edges and printed on the back were his phone number and his name.

Benjamin.

S he and the friend she'd brought as a buffer were standing against a bare brick wall in the back corner of a small bar, sipping whiskey and watching shoes when Benjamin arrived. He emerged through the dark, through the crowd, straight to her, the friend he'd brought for the same purpose as hers trailing behind. A foot in front of her he stopped and said, "Hello."

She reached out and gave him a friendly hug, which immediately felt awkward because they weren't friends and she normally greeted people with a handshake, but he obliged and didn't seem uncomfortable so she tried not to be. The four exchanged introductions and then looked each other over while covering the ways in which they were connected: mutual friends, the café, college majors, artistic tastes.

Benjamin was dressed well, if simply – polished shoes, jeans that fit his thighs, shirt tucked-in and no hat. The details, she noted, had been considered. His cuffs were crisp, jaw clean-shaven, fingernails smooth. He outshined the elements though, appearing perfectly at ease. He stood very still and tall, arms slack at his sides like a presentation, paused and waiting for whatever was next. He didn't fidget or shift his weight and this seemed to make a fool of anyone who wasn't simply comfortable in their own skin. Those people were looking at him and he was looking directly at her.

She waited too, smiling. The minute was amusing. Indeed, what was next? She raised her eyebrows at him. Realizing that she was allowing him to lead, he nodded at her nearly empty drink, stepped away to the bar, and they were off. In order to hear each other above the crowd, they leaned in close over the small table and its slowly emptying glasses. They talked initially about music, which is why they were meeting after all – his music, the city's, in general.

She learned that he built songs from samples of sounds that he either collected or created. Those that he captured might come from dropping cascades of coins on a bare wooden floor, a microphone poised near the point of contact, for example. Those that he created, he might click out from the back of his throat, or draw freehand as a sin wave on a piece of paper. These were then amassed, layered and arranged like a card castle – balanced, towering and complete as a song.

He was an artist. A real one. She was thrilled and relieved.

Next they talked about her work. She wrote. She'd done so obsessively since buying her first diary at a fourth-grade book fair. No scene was too insignificant, though she preferred to illustrate emotions, sensations and intangibles. Colors may be textures, and sounds scents. The aim was always the same: to let her reader sense and see as she sensed and saw. To share the feelings that her dad caused, say.

Words resurrected and immortalized experience. The voracity with which she wrote, she believed was both a product and proof of the practice's responsibility for her survival.

Benjamin and she progressed through family members' names and favorite foods – all presented with unwavering eye-contact, focus forward and attention undivided. Din forced them to repeat details but the frequency and ease of smiles smoothed the breaks in conversation.

Mildly disrupting though were his features, which she remembered from the café but that were much more striking up close and without the protection of a counter between them. His skin was healthy and weathered in the way that youthful skin can be – glowing, not tired. His eyes were enormous and earnest, soft, bright and unblinking. Undistracted, he listened and asked and listened still more yet he wasn't flirting with her … was he? He was so interested in her answers, but he wasn't easy. He pried and then shied, making her come to him. And then he eased and leaned in for more. They discovered that he lived on the same block as she and he knew everyone she knew and together they knew everyone except for each other.

"So," he said, pausing for effect. A question prepared, he took a sip of his drink, swallowed, "Is your boyfriend around?"

She laughed. He waited. Did he know whether she had a boyfriend? She took a sip of her drink, swallowed, "He is around."

They watched each other while all and no words were exchanged, a bit of a dare hanging in the air between. She thought he might get up and walk away and he watched her think this. What was the intent here, now? How did it reflect upon him if he continued on and how did it reflect upon her if she let him? Was this exceptional potential or was it simply indulgent? Smiles may have faded a bit, changing complexions to the seriousness of expression that says: I heard you. Exactly what you said, and everything you didn't. I can tell by your eyes now that you know this. And that what I do or say next – how I react – will be graded by the same hand and with the same caliber that measured your answer just now. Locked eyes held for a second longer and then they both looked away.

Later that night they went dancing. She swallowed her whiskey quicker and tossed her hair. He moved wonderfully. Disarmingly attractive and achingly sexy, he played with the music – alone and happy and so visibly alive – and then with her. Eyes straight into her, he knew the power, wielded it while guiding and then releasing her to move back into selfless company. She tried not to watch him too long.

Her friend told her to, please, she said, at the very least, "You must kiss him."

S he can remember now when they went back to that bar again. She remembers how tightly they held hands and she remembers walking down the narrow hallway to the back, sliding her fingertips along the blank wall that was shaded like everything and everyone else blue-green from a dim light. She remembers him turning around from ahead to look back at her, his eyes veiled and beckoning under a black hat bill.

She remembers, his eyelashes.

And how at the end of the hall, they'd split and walked to opposite sides of the room. People passed between them while they observed each other as the strangers they'd so recently been – recalling the personal and reciprocal singularity that had been given over to an acute partnership. And, they tasted the imminent separation – forced themselves to feel being afar.

She remembers having fought a deep sadness. The shadow snuck up behind her smiles and whispered that it'd known her longer. It lived just behind her heart and protected with severity the softest parts of her insides. A diligent tenant, reinforcing walls and boarding up windows. Her ever escort, it promised to keep her from falling fully, or at least, it'd steal her back in the end, also assuring her that an end existed despite having barely begun. Like an overprotective father or an abusive husband it really did know best. Nemesis or friend, it was trustworthy in its watch. All of this save when it slept and she was left to nearly forget it, thin streaks of light stretching through cracks in the barricade and feeding hope.

They crossed the space and relieved each other by grabbing hands and heading for the door.

She can remember now, having then whispered in his ear that she would remember him there. She would remember the colors and the expressions and the details of his face in the dark.

On Thursday, the day of his album release party, she woke up and sent him a text message that said, *Today is your day*. Later, he told her he'd liked the fact that she'd thought about him first thing in the morning. She'd blushed, not having realized the implication.

That night, she found the club lit red, outside and in. A vague smoke hung at the level of the small paper lanterns that dangled and glowed above the bar – the only sources of light. She arrived alone, ordered a whiskey and stood behind most of the crowd, smoking a cigarette and surveying the scene. She saw him first when he stepped onstage. He didn't look at her, of course not, why should he? She moved nearer the front, though not too close; that would be eager. He introduced his band, himself and then he began to play the music that had enveloped her days ago.

She smiled immediately and tried not to look only at him. His possession of a space, the presence, the ownership of the experience – it was sexy. He was going to subject them all to something – something that he'd created. He was going to drop into it too, along with her and these strangers. They were all going to go somewhere together. Tension and release, all in a set; she felt like a voyeur.

And, she felt awkward for being there, independent among all the friends that had surely known him and the music and his story so much longer. She'd met Benjamin merely three days ago and here she was feeling privy to a discovery. Anxious and assuming (hoping) that he cared that she was there. That he would talk to her. Or more. Everyone else must know the meaning of his lyrics and his muse was probably standing beside her.

She turned on at the force of his breath through the trumpet. Swaying to the music, she lifted her chin above the thickening crowd – drawing nearer the noise and letting the sounds brush her cheeks. She smiled often and ignored the curious glances from other guests maybe wondering who she was, maybe there for the same reason as her, maybe neither.

After the performance, she moved to a dark booth with a mirrored back to chat and be nonchalant. He left the stage into the arms of a line of admirers. She watched him float through them as fluidly as he'd conversed behind the café bar, emerged through the dark on their first meeting, and played with her on the dance floor: easy, comfortable, confident.

Drink, chatter, she jotted some details in her journal, for something to do. When she turned to look for him again, he was sitting beside her.

"Oh," she said, surprised, "Hello."

He held her eye for a second and then answered back, "Hello." Pointed. She felt warmer. He said, "Thank you for coming."

"You're welcome." She prepared to compliment him but he turned to the table and asked how everyone was enjoying the evening. They offered congratulations and praise for the show, which he returned by gifting CDs and buying drinks. Business, of course – he was working tonight. She sat quietly, glancing only once at his hand, which was rested on the arm of her chair. When everyone had been spoken to, he left to attend to the rest of the guests.

Debating departing, she rose and found him blocking her path, his back to her. She touched his shoulder to pass, he turned around and they were pressed into each other by shadows and shoulders. Heat spread across her chest. His fingertips pressed onto her low back, his arm wrapped gently and protectively around her. Her face was at his collar. She could smell him. Inhale. Pause. She stayed very still and sucked down the urge to climb onto him, haul him into her. Exhale. Play. She reached out and placed her palm over his heart, aware that he was watching her. Slow motion. He did not move. She raised her eyebrows first and then her face – slowly up and there he was, eyes directly into hers. Her stomach fell to the floor.

"Um," she said.

He looked amazed. "Hi there."

"I'm just going to …" she nodded at the bar. He didn't look away but he nodded back. She inched off of him lightly, dragging herself out of the pull. Released and shaken she turned around and walked a conscious, straight line away, concealing a grin by keeping her head down. Business. Jesus.

She swallowed a laugh and her pulse vibrated.

That straight line away had not been easy to walk slowly (she could have skipped), and that hold there it had lasted a second and felt like a year – a simple, sensual, natural year.

They left the bar together. Outside on the street, they met a man singing for change. Benjamin dug in his pockets and handed over dollars he'd just made selling his albums. The man extended his arms for a hug and without hesitation Benjamin surrounded him, the visible strength of his embrace surprising her. The man sagged onto a chest offered as square and open as it'd been for her and Benjamin let the dusty hair rest on his shoulder, accepted the hysteric giggles with a hearty laugh and gave an extra squeeze before letting go. Was it a show or was he truly so unreserved with his compassion? The man beamed. And then he reached out to her – more in stumbling gratitude than request.

Startled but obliging, she stepped in and gave it her all – opened her arms wide and let herself be pulled into his musty home of oilcloth layers and knickknack appendages. He was trembling. She held on, keeping her arms strongly around him and trying not to think that by doing so Benjamin might see her as potentially made of the same fiber as he. Even if it turned out that she weren't (though she'd only ever found it to be true that other people were less: less good, sincere or strong), it was easier to back out than to get in. And this was part of the getting in. This was proving something, which is not a disingenuous act.

If Benjamin observed details like she did, it would mean that he was watching now to note whether when she released and stepped back she would be cringing, or grinning. It would also mean that he could have given his hug in as conscious a manner. Had he, where would that put them? Both posturing? Or, both manipulating projections and affecting perceptions? Is intention more significant than action?

So, they'd held on for wrong reasons, but for right ones too – for principle. Regardless of what either noticed or knew about themselves, there remained the man receiving his hugs, and to him that was all that existed in those minutes.

B enjamin drove her home that night. He stopped the car outside of her apartment and through all of the open windows the damp summer dark trickled in to join them. It was dry, moon-bright and clear. The warm air smelled of sweating grass. Without a word, she opened her door and got out, closing it between them before turning around and crouching at the window. Their faces were level. He looked amused by her pause and the deliberate farewell. He, now, was waiting for her.

She said, "I had a wonderful evening, Benjamin."

He said, "I'd like to know more about you."

She swallowed. He held her eye. She said, "Okay."

He was satisfied. "Good night then."

Climbing the steps to her apartment, she was aware of his car continuing up the street to his home, one block away. Her key was nearly in the lock when she stopped. *Wait.* She waited. *Do you feel this?* She grinned, nodded. *Feel this.* She took a step backward. *My.* Dropping her chin to her chest and laughing out loud, she surprised herself with the sound. *To be alive.*

Fingertips to her lips and smiling wide beneath her palm, she looked up at the stars and whispered, "Thank you."

Isabella.

On Friday night he picked her up at seven. His car was freshly clean and she was shy. Isabella wore a dress and kept her legs crossed at the ankle. She was nervous to be on a date and would call it something else, were it anything else. It had been a long time. She felt like an amateur.

He drove quickly. She liked it. There was confidence in the tightly executed corners, alertness at the brief stops and spirit in quick accelerations though gentleness throughout. This was also how he spoke. Directly, with bouts of eagerness, his voice was full and resonant in his throat as he told a little story. He stopped politely when she moved to speak but then jumped in with an enthusiastic interjection. The interruption was endearing, not irritating.

Distracted by self consciousness, she watched his mouth to at least give the impression of following his story. He held his chin high, letting her look at him. He was beautiful. Jaw jutting and square with soft edges under taught suede skin and rough stubble. Cheekbones high below bright eyes and lashes that nearly touched light eyebrows. He looked like a specimen of vitality and fresh manhood – a strapping young gentleman whose mother must be proud. At once he was well-mannered, sexy and innocent. Secure in his body and still young enough to be excited by it. All nerve endings, fingertips and fine hairs that catch the near-brushes of skin, wisps of perfume on wrists and flush in cheeks. A current of energy ran below the still, broad shoulders and she imagined a reigned horse or an idling engine.

Later, she learned that when he turned his full face to you, suddenly you'd find yourself bound and adrift – a body in bondage snug in a chest sunk deep in a bobbing sea. Secure, but possessed. And while he had you captured, he would allow you to see straight through to his innards. As if diving into those eyes, down the throat or spine or however one goes into the depths of another (to the stomach – that's where she imagined the real of people was) you'd reach him. He stood there while you did this, inviting you in, urging you to join him in the clearing. It was an allowance, an opening, that presentation again – the full-frontal unarmed, slow advance – bullets-flying or rubble-underfoot press.

His eyes were wide like children's are. Awed and darting not to avoid but to consume. In their ardent gaze, you were roused the same: teased to excitement right along with him. *Look at the little bird!* Or, *oh, the sky! Look, look quickly now, how beautiful, how funny, how fleeting is this moment of life. Don't you love it? I love it! Love it with me and I will love you.* You'd find yourself too on tiptoe and nodding in agreement *yes, yes!* and then the lid would come off the whole thing, water rushing in, and the two of you would collapse into each other, pockets full of life's perishables.

She noticed the curve of a smile at the corner of his mouth and looked up quickly to see him watching her. Direct and hot, that current leapt into her.

Those are the looks that occur quickly, catching us by surprise like a clap and then we know something is there but it's not yet time to let on so she looked away and kept the conversation light. The second bounced slowly across the back of her brain like an echo and she saw it again, and again, and again as she watched the passing telephone poles.

A rriving at the bar from the first night, they found it inert without its eddied crowds. Sensing that they were still too young in each others' company to be so un-insulated, Benjamin asked if she'd like to go somewhere else – they could return later if they wanted. She said, "Sure."

She said "sure" a lot that night. When they arrived at a darker, warmer bar, she said "sure" to a lavender martini. And then to standing rather than sitting, which is where they stayed, talking for the next several hours. They faced each other while comparing particulars and the lines on their palms. People slowly filling in the fringes edged them closer.

He bowed near to emphasize a point and she stood her ground. He gestured wide with his arms and she, teetering a bit on her heels, swayed with him. He said he'd always noticed her delicate ankles. She eyed him and he held hers relentlessly – not looking at her lips or her breasts or around the room. She was flustered by the undivided attention and reveled in it tentatively. His patience was challenging. Listening intently to every word, his pace suggested that he would continue to do so as long as it took to know her. Subjects were not skimmed, they were exhausted.

When it was her turn to tell a story, she embarked boldly but allowed herself to become wrapped up in it, excited, only to a point – unable to let go of that precious (cursed) composure. When she felt self-conscious, she returned the topic to him and though he accepted her bashfulness, his focus remained unwavering. Answering her question thoroughly, losing himself in an anecdote (she observed exactly how he expanded on details, described a scent, took his time), he always returned gracefully, landing solidly on his feet and passing the play back to her.

With each reply, she tried to better take her time, share more. This was new for her, this exercise in unguardedness.

Indulging confidence, she wound down to a low voice, and with her words precise and pronounced, rolling sensually off of her tongue and lips, licking and hovering, she pulled him in and then finished with a shrug, an arched eyebrow, a sideways glance and a sip of her drink.

One beat. He grinned. Two. He let out a full laugh and tossed back his head. She got him. She laughed too.

As the night progressed, they seesawed and mirrored. Encouraged and contagious they found matched jests, sympathies and an easy playfulness. It was like a dance of finesse and character. A waltz of intimacy, honesty and frivolity: to share enough about oneself in the appropriate time and manner to be rightly received. Every eye-contact counted, all actions of the hands considered. And while knowing that these movements are being observed, to appear not to. Or, perhaps, to reveal just enough recognition to show awareness, but not self-absorption. Your companion doing the same.

I am poised. I know I am poised, but I am not entirely trained – some, much of this is inherent. I am perceptive but also confident enough not to always know or care if you are watching. I see what you are looking at; I might know what you are thinking. Do you know what I am thinking? I will give you a clue with my eyes – now.

She found this acuity inseparable from the precarious process of opening herself.

They familiarized each other's faces. She sought flaws in the façade, red flags or inconsistencies but all she found was him watching her for the same. Isabella reminded herself that intelligent people, capable of communicating, did exist, which would make her a fool for feeling so flattered. He pushed into her with a look that stopped her thought. Were he speaking, she'd have heard: *I am uncommon. I will show you.* She dug her heels into the floor and raised that chin. His eyes flashed. She gave in, bit, set down her drink to clasp her hands behind her back and let it bubble out of her: "I like you," she said.

He stepped across the space and swept her into a hug. That was not what she'd hoped for.

"I like you too," he said.

She didn't want to come on too strong but maybe he couldn't tell she was just aching to kiss him.

He pulled away, leaving her with a breeze and the chasm between them was nearly impossible not to tumble into. Out of it she surfaced like from a hot bath – aroused but unsteady. Mindful of its intoxication, she yielded to the seduction of the week.

It was time to go. Somewhere else at least. A standoff now felt explicit – the challenge direct and daring. The one to shy would be the coward. Halfway to the other bar he asked if she'd like to go to the beach instead.

She said, "Sure."

They bought syrah at a convenience store and with the bottle in one hand and his shoes in the other, he led her along the rocky spine of the beach. Dry weeds, seemingly sleeping, stroked their ankles as they passed. Silhouettes stretched and yawned. The air was the temperature of her skin and the sand warmer. The water whispered to the shore and the dunes murmured behind them. The watchful moon shone brightly above, illuminating only as much of their surroundings as they need see. The languid night wrapped protectively around them, excluding time.

She opened the wine with a screwdriver stolen from the glove box of the car and the force of shoving the cork into the neck exploded grape blood drops, invisible in the dark, onto their cheeks. Benjamin and Isabella took turns sipping from the bottle and speaking carefully, voices lower and rawer now in the violet hour.

Sitting with them was the hot suspense of the impending. Strung and stretching thinner with every swallow and playful nudge, their knees are touching now. It hummed. When they turned to speak they were face to face – lips and eyes aligned. The pitch rose. She was liquid and then vapor. Hands gripping the earth, every nerve was alight with life and receiving. She was edgy with anticipation and elated to be young, and to know it – to be present. The want for more mixed equally with the contentment of enough. *Show me, teach me, take me.* It was about to snap.

Right then, he was her greatest love – the man of her dreams. He was the future because he was the present and only there does the future exist. In that eternal minute, he was limitless and infallible, and so was she. Before anything, they were everything because they might be.

She was nearly bursting and it was going to be her move. He was allowing only, not advancing, respecting obviously her mark in the sand. To leap or to revel in the fear of heights and the view from the top? To cross the center line? Ah, but, she thought, *all's fair in –*

She leaned in and he met her with full, soft lips pressed entirely over hers. He reached to her face and didn't allow her to pull back. She climbed onto him and –

and they kissed red wine mouths together, put sandy hands on bare skin. His scooped her hair and held the back of her neck firmly. She inhaled his breath, took his bottom lip between her teeth, opened her eyes. He wrapped a strong arm around her ribs, pulling her against him. Her mouth beside his ear, she let him hear her trembling breath. He pushed her aside and then straddled her, pinning her wrists with his knees. He pressed his mouth hard on hers – his reply. She listened by letting him. He whispered something into her lips and she said, *sure, sure, yes.*

And so: Isabella saw phosphorescence for the first time in her life that night. Electric glitter water that flickered when she pushed her fingers into it, tickled as it swirled around her naked thighs and scurried ahead of his hands when he reached for her below the invisible surface. It slid down their shoulders in glowing streaks and streamed from their fingertips and elbows in live little drips of light. Around their hips it ricocheted with the excitement of an unexpected intrusion, interruption of the usual. Something, something, something was happening – titter, titter, chirrup.

L ater, Isabella is sitting alone in her New York City apartment writing this story. Every evening she dims all but a single light, clears off the surface of her desk and puts on his CD. Then she leaves the room, closing the door gently behind her and padding down the hall to the bathroom where she patiently washes her face and brushes her teeth, her mind on the tiny chamber behind her that is steadily filling with the notes of history. When she reenters the room, she does so delicately – going directly to the lone chair that remains in position from nights past. She sits, erect but tender, hands dropped by her sides and fingertips stretched toward the floor. Sucking in the sweetened air, she rolls her shoulders back, lifts her chin and lets the mist settle on her forehead.

Allowing to rise what will, the surge is steady and it tugs at the tiny hairs on her arms. She closes her eyes as her body lightens, lifts. She feels like a sail full of static-electric air – a vessel suspended. A wave washes over her, delivering memories like low-tide debris. Amid the shimmering collage she sees his hands at the piano, on her thighs, there are tears on her pages.

Their affair unravels in letters and sentences before her. She is pinning butterfly wings. And now her neck is wet.

They'd sped down so many dark highways, speechless and too deeply aching to breathe right. Crippled in their seats. Both passengers. They were unable to comprehend more than that it afflicted them equally. The mutuality both afforded relief and exacerbated the experience. The third dimension was god and their child – a responsibility, a force and a test of human capacity to commit. It had all come at them from of nowhere.

Two cars head-on colliding in a glorious crash. Wreckage raining as glass snow around bodies broken but breathing. From the mixed parts and mingled blood, what would emerge? Would there be life or ruin? Where would they be when they reached their destination?

W hen she woke up, he was gone. Perched on the edge of his bed, she placed her feet in a square of sunlight on the wood floor and touched sand that had followed them home the night before.

It felt as if he'd left the room only minutes ago. A glass of orange juice, half full, sat on the dresser. A drawer was open, a t-shirt hanging on its corner. Every few seconds a drop of water escaped a faucet she could not see and the tiny splashing sound tinkled out into the silence. The objects, his possessions, his home was roosted and curious. As was she. The blankets below her palms patiently waited for her rise so that they might refill with the day's fresh air. She stood and they inhaled.

Dressed, she inspected the refrigerator and then went to his desk. Above it hung a bulletin board, flaking and laden – a pinned patchwork quilt with scraps of the past and directions for the future. The largest note, written in black marker on red construction paper declared: "Do not be fooled by the intensity of taboo."

She reached out to lift one of the layers but stopped with her hand outstretched. Particles sparkled in the air between her fingertips and a photo. Tiny bits of the dust had landed and frosted a fine layer on the picture. She took back her hand slowly to leave the air unmoved, imagining the ripples of her fingerprint on the photo had she touched it. In years the ripples would have become waves, washing the color from the corner of the memory. Her contact would have left a vacant stain on a reminiscence she wasn't a part of. The mark a rude reminder of her invasion – a broken blade of grass, a scar, a one-night stand. She put her hands in her pockets and continued looking.

She was in photos on a board just like this one. It hung in her apartment that very minute. She was the other half of the couple with their cheeks pressed together, saying, *Look mom! We're really doing it.* She was the girl on her back in the grass at the park, drinking beer in the sun instead of studying. Her fingerprints were on those negatives. In the earliest photo she is blowing out candles on her 18th birthday. The boy had sneaked a message to the waiter that it was her celebration and then he'd taken the photo so that she would have some token from their simple celebration. It was the summer after high school graduation. They'd become friends on the last day of school and passed two muggy months in all-night conversations about religion and fathers. The sexual tension had made her belly ache for the days until one night they'd gotten drunk on jug wine and over a game of cards he confessed to having fallen in love with her. She took him to the floor and from then on, they were together – a pair of presumptuous mavericks.

In another photo, they are facing each other on an old couch in her even older dorm. It was their first day of college and they're grinning at each other like, *This is going to be a piece of cake.* Then, she is in his sweatshirt, lying in his bunk bed. Not visible in the photo is what she carved into the boards above their heads: "Life is beautiful." That was the night she took his virginity. Next, they're standing in the empty bedroom of their first apartment, proud. Behind them is a mattress, their only piece of furniture. They never did get a bed frame, but they made a home together, rode bikes to class together and hosted sweaty house parties. Ants toured the kitchen in single-file lines and they fought over who should do dishes, but when someone stole her bike, he found it and stole it back for her. He'd pushed it into the den with shoulders tossed back and his head high. He was a good boyfriend.

A year later everything felt too small, the walls too close and the home too much like, well, home. The apartment she moved into next, alone, was closer to her favorite café and had a view of everyone else through a wall of sunset-facing windows. She could see downtown from her bed and every night she would whisper, *Good night city.*

She found the apartment by way of a boy she'd met at one of the parties. He was frighteningly eccentric, disappearing for months at a time and trembling when he spoke, which he did less often than he scribbled in the little black notebook that never seemed to leave his hands. She grabbed it from him once, when no one else was looking, and wrote in it: *I want you to fall in love with me.*

He did. One night thereafter, she lied to her boyfriend about being too drunk to make it home in order to spend the night with him. He'd given her his bed – a broken futon on the floor – and his only blanket. Zipping himself into a jacket and pulling the sleeves pulled out over his hands, he wrapped his arms around himself and lay on the carpet next to her with wide eyes. Never touching her but also never sleeping, he admired her face with heartbreaking awe and whispered finally, definitively when the sun rose, that she was drawn of "fucking excellent lines".

Soon, she was spending all of her free time hidden away with him in the little studio in the sky, cutting up fashion magazines and making grand plans. He photographed her in parks and called her Dolly and when he left for Paris, she took over the apartment. She'd also sat on the curb in front of her old home for hours. Five hours actually, waiting for her boyfriend to come home and when he did, she cried and he listened to her and said okay. They got back together and continued on. Diligently she maintained their wall of memories as if there'd been no interruption. The ticket stubs and cookie-fortunes on the bulletin board to which she belonged had been collecting for three and a half years.

How old was the collage in front of her now? Whose life was this?

And then she saw it – a clean triangle of creaseless white paper. It was pinned near the middle, on top of everything. Printed carefully in pencil were her first name and her telephone number. This was the fingerprint she'd not wanted to make just minutes before but it would leave a hole if she stole it back. It would be remembered. She was now present among all the unfamiliar characters in another life story – his. Cast. She drank the rest of the glass of juice and went home.

She took a shower and changed her clothes, all the while in wonder about what was happening. Her head hurt. Though, that was no matter. She'd just had a night she'd remember forever. This was the morning after. Some part of her had changed.

On her way out the door, she grabbed a sheet of paper and a blue crayon, which is all she could find to write with in her hurry back to Benjamin. She wrote a note, folded it in half and stuck it under the driver's side windshield wiper of his car on her way back to the café.

Benjamin,

It has been a terrifying pleasure getting to know you.

The world shifted — I can feel it — and I love it.

This is going to be great.

B enjamin sat beside her while she sipped her coffee. She felt vulnerable in the harsh sunlight. A rag was tossed over his shoulder and though wearing his apron again, he wasn't serving anyone but her. As usual, she was observing his manner of attentiveness. It let him come at you right through things – directly up against her in an unobstructed way. It was very naked. And then she had the wonderful realization that she knew what he looked like naked.

Casual, she wanted to be casual; it was no big deal that they'd slept together. No expectations. She hoped he didn't have any.

He put his hand on her knee, "Are you okay? I mean, with last night?"

His usual audience of friends and coworkers watched from a distance.

"Yeah." She smiled. "Last night was fun."

"Good." He hesitated.

She watched him, waiting and appreciating his company. He could have remained behind the bar, offered a wave or a complimentary coffee, but rather he'd rounded the counter and was here making that face like: *Do you mind that I'm touching you? I know we're in public, but I don't care if they see; I want to touch you. I mean, unless you mind ...*

Her Americano was perfect. It tasted like baked soil and chicory.

He said, "Would you like to meet my parents?"

She said, "Sure." And so, that afternoon Benjamin and Isabella were together atop glittering water. Boating away from the shore, throttle out and wind stinging their eyes they tore a white-edged rip down the middle of the picture, sending out wide waves in every direction. Isabella was delirious with the adrenaline and confusion of having been broadsided by another body; one that felt celestial, but was male – complete, complementary and encompassing. Still, she held on to her seat and did not say *slow down* because this was a contest of wits and she would not be beaten nor sacrifice whatever prize winning was to fear or exhaustion.

Walking through the front door of his family home, she felt as if she were returning to her own. There was more light than furniture and the near-scent of coffee, as if from the café where they'd been sitting mere hours ago. The ambience was consciously tranquil and casually elegant. A Turkish rug greeted her in the entry and in its corner a stack of shoes was piled pigeon-toed and askew. She removed her own. Benjamin stepped out of his, toe-to-heel, leaving them empty in midstride behind him. The elements of the house were all so seemly that Isabella had to make a point to notice them in her search for peculiarities, which yielded none. Just enough trinkets lined the countertops, the couch was well-loved and the water view through the living-room windows said, *you may only think you've seen this before.*

In front of her spread the foyer, its color palette immediately familiar. Mauve and teal throws matched brush strokes in the wall art that was framed with the same dark wood as the coffee table. On it a vase overflowed with hodge-podge flowers obviously cut from plants in the yard not arranged by an expert. Isabella imagined her own mother's daisy-printed gardening gloves clutching sturdy rose stems that let foamy white blood from the tips of their sliced slants. She realized that she was at ease, and then became shaken – offended that it had snuck up on her here within others' walls. Assuming where the bathroom was, she went there to repeat his parents' names to herself in the mirror while applying eye drops, splashing water on her face and closing an extra button on her blouse.

When introduced to his mother and father, she spoke properly, clinging to composure and all of her manners that she might pass the test that meeting the parents is, is, is. But, they greeted her less cautiously than she expected, bowling over her soft speech as if she must be pretending to be shy, and hugging across her extended hand. Their faces were bright and open, their handshakes firm and their eye-contact as steady as their smiles. Rows of their twinkling-white teeth were reflected by a bank of family photos on the mantle. Isabella nearly recognized the cheeks, grins and hair color of the cousins. She could have known them already; they didn't look like strangers but rather like relatives she might have met as a child and not seen since. However, she didn't know them, just as she'd not known the fans at Benjamin's show or the past on his bulletin board. She was brushed aside by the breadth of the bond between kin. He was theirs. She refrained from touching him in front of them.

The parents led the cautious couple to the living room, seated them on the window-facing couch and took the opposite, facing the closed front door.

Benjamin's album played softly in the background and the sun kept watch through skylights above the scene. Because Benjamin knew little more than how Isabella took her coffee, he could not tailor her introduction. He wasn't able to share that about her of which he was most proud; he didn't yet know how she complimented him or what they did together for fun. This was risky. Isabella was impressed by his apparent faith in her answers as well as his parents' un-skeptical acceptance of their son's decision to bring home this stranger-girl. They smiled kindly, taking in the pair with well-concealed befuddlement and then naturally took the lead, as adults who are versed in conversations without context or comfortable where youth may not be, can. Gently, they pried, suggested and posed – Benjamin and Isabella's features taking shape as if under a sculptors thumb.

Isabella could feel the pressure of the unlikelihood of their separate selves continuing to connect as well as they had in the few quick hours they'd opened up to each other. By the firmness of his hold on her hand, she supposed that he must too. She realized through the unpreparedness of the exchange that he hadn't invited her on a trip he'd intended to make anyway; she was the purpose for it. And all the while he was there, fumbling his way half-blindly through the hours alongside her. While she kept her fingertips pressed into the wall for balance, he held on to her wrist.

His parents had met as children, and then again in the military. After a series of near misses, including his mother's short engagement to a pig farmer, they passed three intensely romantic weeks in Italy and then wed. They endured his slow-starting career and her weight challenges while raising three exemplary children. As parents, they were an enthusiastic, unruly, inexhaustible pair that could fall and wriggle on the rug right along with the toddlers, leaving the video camera to run on its side. They emerged triumphant with a home full of flat-screen televisions, a basement of boxed holiday decorations and the childhood cat. He let her paint polka dots on the front porch, she laughed at his puns and they kissed when no one was watching. They organized frequent family reunions, conducted sing-alongs and were the last of the party to sleep. Atop each family tree sat a great grandmother spit-and-vinegar. The lineage met at his parents and from them burgeoned arms of nieces, nephews and loyally inducted in-laws. The love and respect was formidable.

All of the children were obvious effects of this support: confident, creative and bold. Benjamin had two sisters – what he considered the perfect kid-ratio and the opposite of what Isabella favored. He got along with them and his mother, and females in general, famously. The health of his relationship with women came from a genuineness and respect that was less of equality than favoritism for the other gender. Isabella knew about this and she knew what his sisters had taught him because she herself was a sister. She knew how he felt amid girls because she was most comfortable as one of the boys. This equivalency made her feel masculine beside him, and too, him feminine. He crossed his legs unselfconsciously at the knee while laughing and gesturing. She remained still, low-voiced and calm. Like an undertow she settled him. And he, a lively flood, swept her into levity, encouraging girlishness. She became the giddy one and then their roles felt suited and they looked at each other and smiled with a satisfied, self-aware sort of realization that this was good.

After the introductions, Benjamin and Isabella stole away to the dock to kiss. Through hard-pressed lips and hands on cheeks, she could feel that his need to confirm was as urgent as hers. One sense, at least, required reassurance. Relieved, they shot accusing stares at each other, straightened their shirts and walked back up the gravel trail to the house. She thought it was time to go home but he said,

"My parents would love it if we stayed for dinner. Let's?"

The path below her feet became transparent. Layers of duplicates unfolded under and on either side of her. Sunlight blistered around the leaves, burning spots in her vision. A flanking wall of trees turned to phantoms and then so did she. The wind blew through her and the horizon skewed sharply. Branches swung at her from the left and then she realized that they were far in the distance. A web of gnats poured onto her face but when she went to brush them away, there were none. A large black bird dove low overhead, casting a shadow on the earth that she wished would simply hold still so that she could walk. His voice was traveling miles to reach her – a mimic of his question bouncing off of tunnel walls. She could only nod in reply, knowing that the sound of her words traveling the same way as his would cause her heart to pitch with fear, throwing her to that brink beyond which was imminent death or insanity. There she would teeter, so close to losing something, everything, it.

She'd always had a vague fear of losing touch with reality. Like, when at that edge, feeling the reeling of the planet, she had to grip fistfuls of grass else her feet lift from the land or her mind simply float away like a stray balloon.

She made herself breathe slowly and she made herself smile, hoping that the small movements in her face might trick her body into producing happier chemicals. She cooed to herself silently, *Shh, you're okay. It's okay. Everything will be all right. Hush.* She imagined being rocked gently back and forth. Ironically, the way to regain control was to relinquish it – to pretend like you don't know that this is a bluffing game and to play along long enough to become convinced by the other reality that is no more actual than the upsetting one. It's really impossible to let go knowing that you are, but this is necessary for survival.

Isabella continued walking, using him for balance and not letting him know that anything was wrong – hiding it well beneath only a flushed cheek. She looked around, trying to orient herself as upright and appreciate the pleasantness of the setting in order to return it to serene from severe. The panic came in rushes that crashed onto her from the side, washing over her eyes and obscuring straight lines like a circus mirror. Currents surged up her spine as if she were wrapped in the arms of an electric jellyfish, turning her to a trembling wreck, mast swaying. She felt helpless and blind and deaf and alone. Both at the mercy and singularly capable of saving herself – her own death and rescue. She held her breath through the tumble, trusting, knowing, hoping she'd come out of it.

And it worked; she slammed into stillness. The surroundings caught up with her sight too slow but at least she could see. The wind rested and time was missing from the day anyway so she quit trying to catch it and said, "Sure."

The parents had opened wine. From his father, she accepted a glass and from his mother, the vase of flowers from the living room. Each with a hand on her back, the jovial two showed the way to a table set with paper plates and plastic forks outside under the sunset. Isabella was relieved to see the day's wane.

Fighting the dread into the back of her throat and wondering how she would swallow food past the choke, she told his mother that everything looked delicious. The sound of her own voice pushed her back toward the edge and her heart ticked on toward bursting. Sitting down, she put one hand between her thighs and pressed them tightly together, holding onto herself. Oh it was agony! Stupid anxiety. She tortured herself; it ached in her belly, in her shivering everything. She sipped her wine knowing and too grateful to be slightly sad that it would help.

Only able to focus in one place at a time, she moved through the meal in stop-motion. Dishes, faces and words entering and exited the blurry-edged frame. A salad bowl full of fluffy green leaves souped in white dressing and specked with black pepper arrived from her right. A pitcher of water, ice cubes clinking and condensation frosting its bust approached her from across the table. She moved her glass to accept a pour and a crystal drop of water fell from its base, running across her knuckles like its sibling drips had done in hundreds the night before. The bustle of eating commenced and Benjamin took the conversation to himself – doling out the details that feed parents' pride. The delighted two lapped up his presence with unmasked ownership. From the mother: he is her creation on display; from the father, he is a flesh connection to youth. Benjamin spoke about his life with abandon, causing his role to waver between adult (surprising Isabella by not omitting personal details she'd never have shared with parents) and excited child with an unabashed eagerness to please them. By now, she knew that his gregariousness was characteristic. Its oft emergence made her happy and comfortable. It was endearing if a bit clumsy. Rather than reservation, he was inclined to whims of fancy. There was honesty in the innocence and a sensitivity that she could imagine needing to be near. However unstable the spontaneity, it was also a welcome assault to the strictness of her posture.

The party raised glasses to toast their son's visit, and just before the clinks, his mom added: "Oh, what the hell, welcome to the family!" completing the cheers. Benjamin coughed and Isabella laughed though she could have cried, so entirely displaced and confused and yet somehow nothing felt wrong.

The scene revolved once or twice more and then Isabella realized that she and Benjamin were alone. He was beside her but looking away so she blew a soft breath at his neck – a long, gentle exhale that silently whispered across the space between them. With that breath went the last of her fear. With it went all the grip from her muscles. With it she relaxed, released, and the clock on the wall resumed its ticking. As the last bits of air tickled off of his neck he straightened and she knew that they were reconnected and replaced in the present. By doing this, she was marking the page. By reaching out and touching him, she caught his attention and the moment became mutual and so would live – its life ensured by their memories.

He smiled and turned to her, understanding. Her face was easy. They saw each other clearly and all stilled and widened and she was warm.

It was dark when they left and on impulse they drove straight to her mother's house. It seemed only fair. They accepted tea for uneasy stomachs, hoping to soothe the absolute exhilaration that rushed through their veins to tingling extremities. It was pushing to an end though, the night growing shorter despite their resistance, their staying – staying awake, staying together, staying in motion.

He sat down at the piano on which her grandmother, her mother, and she had learned to play. Resting his hands on the keys, he gently pressed one down, and then another. A melody rose up around them, haunting and tentative, crouching and ominous. It suggested, and then replied, asked again and resolved with a *Who knows?* Isabella's eyes welled with tears. Her mother asked what it was and Benjamin said he didn't know, it'd just come to him then. He said he would call it The Bella Melody.

In exchange for his performance, he asked to hear her read. So, she carried out an armful of essays and loose pages. There were so many to choose from in her library of scribbles, sentences and stories. Papers, worn black moleskins and dear diaries that chronicled her childhood had been filled with something new nearly every day, though rarely shared with anyone. At the top of the first page, in the indent before the first word, Isabella halted, speechless and nervous. She doubted her talent, especially following his, which was definite, titled and validated. She simply wrote and she always had. She wrote like she breathed – like she came in contact with and consumed. She wrote to experience, to see, to feel and to understand. She wrote too to save – to remind herself what it felt like to be there, then and here, now. But, despite that her life effectuated the identity, in her opinion this didn't give her permission to promote it, to claim the craft or assume it would have her. Nor, she thought, should she subject others to it or suggest that they should consider her words among those who really wrote.

These words though, might possibly be why she was here. So, they did deserve more respect – the opportunity to also breathe, a chance. If they be palatable only to her, or cost her this show then so be it. For them, for the girl who had made them, and so lived to tell and to best that blasted fear (she couldn't stop now), she leapt into the line. There was immediate relief among the letters and though her voice wavered, her pace and pronunciation through the paragraphs was precise. Rolling over the sentences' structures like a slow clicking train along its tracks, she felt the solidity and trusted it – herself.

The End was a *Who knows?* and after three seconds of silence, he said, "Isabella, you are great."

The blood rushed to her cheeks and fresh air to her lungs. He said, "Oh what a relief, you're great!" And so was he. They stared at each other and their minds ran toward hope from hesitation as they climbed another rung up this ride, higher into the sky.

Finally, they drove home. And went straight to his bed to hide in exhausted relief under the muting heaps of blankets with only a safe circle around them illuminated by lowly flickering candles that he lit naked. She looked at his body: the flat abdomen with soft hair circling the belly button and thickening as it descended. His thighs were lean and strong and the inners brushed each other where everything seemed to come together in a jumbled triangle below his narrow hips. He held the matches between his fingertips and maneuvered a votive upside-down over the flame to catch the wick while not suffocating it nor dripping wax on the floor near his bare feet. She watched him climb onto the bed, pausing above her – looking down at her and letting her look at him before falling beside her and wrapping his arms and legs around her. She found his hands and feet with her own and just before falling asleep, she put her lips by his ear and inhaled.

S unday morning they woke up sober. She was alert with anxiety that was not soothed by the softness of the blankets and the warm weight of him pressed against her back. He awoke startled, minutes after her and they eyed each other with an interest in the sensations of simultaneous camaraderie and self-consciousness from sharing a morning routine with a stranger: a girl watching a boy lather himself with soap, a boy watching a girl wrap her hair in a towel. She observed the order in which he dried his body after stepping out of the shower (left his back wet, the water evaporating by the time he had selected a shirt). Too, she was aware of how she clasped her bra and buttoned her jeans.

They readied quietly, keeping their voices gentle and their touches tender as if nursing bruises, checking health and testing the steadiness of the ground beneath their feet. While he brushed his teeth, she faced him in the mirror and told a story:

When she was a young girl, her dad had owned a small black bullet of a sports car. On special occasions, he'd take her and her two younger brothers out for rides. And rides they were. At his hands, corners were as sharp as his words, stops abrupt like slaps and the accelerations suffocating. The speed flattened her skinny chest against the stiff leather seat and she imagined that the highway shot right through her. Through the sunroof, the tops of trees smeared into the sky.

Isabella was sure that with every turn, the car would lift and roll, turning her little family into a tumbling mess of limbs and torn t-shirts. She watched this scene like a load of drying laundry. She would have been at fault for its happening. The mass of the speed was heavy like the weight of that guardianship but she never asked her dad to slow down because he was even more frightening than the course. Her role was muting, which allowed her to appear fearless. And in that silence was secret relief – a forced freedom and irresponsibility. He was in control, even if it was of taking their lives with the wheel under his thick fingers. Aggressively he maneuvered the sleek machine to his will, which apparently was not to rear and fly, kill. Ever since those drives, she'd received a searing cheer as a passenger in speeding cars. Her bust always accepted the familiar pressure as a relished replacement for what was ever else there. Speed threw her half in front of herself and half behind – shoved through her shoulder blades and through the seat. There she was happily separated, split in two and exempt from the present by being before it, and after. Suspended and nowhere quite, she was moving too quickly to be anywhere. Until it all snapped back into place.

Her brothers and she rated the speeds in colors. Pink speed was the slowest. Black speed was the fastest.

She blinked and they left for breakfast.

T hey sat at the center of a wide, open restaurant. In air saturated lightly with hash brown grease they held hands over a red-checked tablecloth, yellow pats of butter and blue backed menus. Around their still table spun slowly the cushioning bustle and clinking of brunch – an hour that is a pocket in time, stretching morning through afternoon and showing leisure and laze in oozing egg yolks and ever half-full cups of coffee. Syrup-soaked bread sopped around others' plates and mashed in their mouths between church discussion or weekend recall. The waitress arrived above their table apron-first with a prepared white notepad and lots of other customers to serve.

Benjamin ordered coffee and Isabella chamomile tea because she'd been shaking since they met. They both ordered omelets and toast with extra jam. She wanted to hide in his arms but she didn't even know him. And that's why they were there; she was going to decide now to either know him, or never to know him. She had all and the only authority to make that decision. Once again, everything was waiting for her. The world behind a door, the race beyond a starting line, the confrontation of a reality that seemed to have skipped them for the weekend.

It was Sunday, which was a day away from Monday, and it would all either be real or left as a dream by then. So, they took back their hands and started talking. Stumbling through "I like you", they laughed a little at the obviousness and release it afforded. Then, of course, she had to talk about her relationship – the one that she was in with someone else. She had to answer that a week ago she'd been happy and in love and blind to the prospect of anything else. Now this … and she couldn't just … but as she said this, she already didn't own the words.

Her ideas were ahead and excitement was rising and she wasn't afraid.

He looked at her through the tea steam and without a sideways glance, he leaned across the table and said,

"Do you want to do this?"

She shouldn't have but she believed he really could do it. It didn't make any sense, it was unreasonable, and so much was unknown. He couldn't possibly be as great as he seemed and even if he were, it didn't necessarily allow him to know her, or what he was getting himself into. She didn't doubt that she could love him – that, she imagined was the easier part. Should she spare him? Maybe they'd gone too quickly – falling for the falling, liking the idea, loving being in love. Her mind ran this way and that and he said,

"Hey."

She stopped and let sneak forward the tender *What if?* The thought that had been hiding under the mad-flying others, reassured by his still gaze and that he didn't seem to doubt this. Or, if he did, it was irrelevant. More important was his duty to seize the moment, bring her home, to not say, *slow down*. Like the landscape beyond a carousel, the clip of the city revolving outside of the restaurant slowed, windows clicking closer to an alignment, suspense in where they might stop.

The *maybe* was so small. She knew she could crush it. She knew she could say goodbye to him there and walk away, continue on her way and let the weekend have been merely frivolous. That would be safe. She would ache some for him and wonder now and then but she could lose that with time.

She looked back at him and he was watching patiently with an expression that suggested he knew. How did he always seem to? This was new. There was something in him that she'd never seen before. She saw a man. Not a boy, she saw someone who might understand her in a way she'd not been before. He was strong and sure and straight and he was himself purely and boldly and he was sitting there across the table from her wanting her to let him. He might give her great things. She suspected that he offered a life larger than she could live any other way, at least as far into the future as she could or needed to see from here.

Isabella knew what was going to happen next. She was sure before she'd thought every one of her thoughts though she let them have their time in her mind else she feel completely irrational. Now, it was her turn to wait, which she did in contentment, barely sitting now, the warmth sliding up in her elbows and the back of her knees, distracting her from the thoughts that filled and burst like thin bubbles, misting her forearms. And before the food had even arrived she was on the edge of her chair, hands squeezed in her lap, readying her lips and her throat, thinking *what the hell* and *this is life* and *you have to* and *going is always the answer* and securing his eyes she nodded, nodded, laughed and said,

"Yes."

He said, "Black speed."

B enjamin and Isabella stood on the sidewalk between their two apartments, facing each other in chipper morning air. She was uneasy. That day they separated for the first and last time (until the final time). They separated so that they could be together. She was going to find and leave her boyfriend. Benjamin eclipsed her view. A sharp shadow cut across his chest. The sun, blocked by the corner of the apartment building behind her sliced a crisp diagonal line over his t-shirt. It began near his heart and dropped over his ribs, wrapping around his right waist. His lower half was shrouded in darkness that covered his feet and hers too in a pool of shade. They were rooted in this, emerging from the same something. The top half of him – and god, the great blue sky behind and above was blindingly bright. She winced like *yes, yes, I'm awake, and I see, it is clear, I get it.*

Though she couldn't rationally know quite how she could see more with a stranger, which was like seeing nothing at all, Isabella had a feeling, a belief – perhaps her first experience with faith. She knew the direction, but not the destination. This was an enormity that was all potential, but just that. The later regret of having not attempted this unknown was surer than the reward of remaining in the known. This was also accepting that because she had chosen to make it the law of her life not to pass possibility of this magnitude, flights like this, magnificent roller coasters would rise up, and she would ride them. And she would be afraid, and feel sick, and maybe be sick, but she would survive or die in motion. From her fibers, she'd always known that this was how the stages in her life would advance. Leaping for its own sake is an obligation of us alive and able and with any palate for experience.

This way wouldn't come without its consequences. She would lose some things, and cause a casualty, but the wager was for good, best, better in the end. It may be running from something (fear of that regret), or it may be simple fearlessness. Either way, Isabella's position was similar to her spot in the car beside Dad on their drives: someone else sat behind the wheel and so she was forced to go. The requisite silence made cowardice and courageousness indistinguishable. Representing now her future self and upholding a responsibility to her by setting a precedent to live assertively, she was committed to this impulse. Her path had already been decided; the first step was now only waiting to be taken. And she would take it. It was one of the things in life that you simply did. You said yes because if you didn't, you weren't really living – you were watching the living. You leapt, you said *sure*, you went. Which meant:

She was going to break someone's heart today. She was going to assault someone innocent and unsuspecting. She was going to change someone's life today. She was going to rearrange his future and extract herself, slowly and gently from every memory they'd intended to make together. She was going to catch him completely off guard and he would hurt and cry and hate her. He wasn't going to understand. He would beg and plead for her not to go.

Benjamin was saying something about being strong for her. She heard it, felt confused and returned to the present. *What?* She was skeptical that someone could mean this, that they would offer it, and that she would believe it. She didn't understand the experience of trusting. She was who she relied on. Yet, she wouldn't learn if she didn't proceed. So, she was already in mid-air and if it wasn't water that was below her, well, it wouldn't matter how much she needed or wanted it to be.

Benjamin caught her chin with his fingertips and lifted her face, directing her eyes to his. He held her shoulders and told her again like repeating to a child: He'd do anything in his power – he was here for her – he was hers – whatever she needed.

She laughed.

He didn't.

She sighed and opened her arms, accepting his hug with her cheek on his chest and her breath out into the day.

They parted and she started walking. Just walking. She set a steady pace and headed down the street, turning left at the bottom of the hill toward the water that was miles away. She chose directions without thinking, letting stoplights and wind lead the way. Cars passed, the shrubs along the roadside grew and shrank, bowing in and out of her path. The air grew hot and sweat tickled down the backs of her knees. Gritty leftover sand in her shoes rubbed her feet raw and the tops of her shoulders burned. She didn't feel much, simply walking, watching pass what did and following each step with her mind, equal and methodical. She noted the breeze on her forearms and kept her palm on the cell phone in her purse, waiting for the right time to call. She came to the water and had to choose: north or south. She dialed her boyfriend's phone number, turned north, and waited until he picked up before continuing on.

Not sure how to begin, she said,

"Hey. So, where are you?" She wanted to find him so that they could speak in person. She thought she might be able to explain it better that way. He could see that this was sincere and she'd cry and so would he and he'd fight against her but she'd have some hold on the situation, putting herself in front of him – not hiding, not that she was. She could ease him down gently.

Knowing something immediately, he said, "No." He said, "Tell me now."

She wasn't ready. She was afraid. "No."

"Yes." And, it was really up to him anyway.

She was sad to do it this way. She asked, "Are you sure?"

"Yes. Tell me now."

What does one say?

She said, "I've met someone else." And she realized that she may never see his face again.

"Oh my god," he said. "Please tell me you're joking."

Over their disassembly, the sun peaked, and sank, and set. The sweat dried on her neck and her body tired hours before the end.

He said he hated her. And that: she was weak. She was distracted by shiny things. She was ripping his heart out. Everyone would love her, but no one knew her – not really, not like he did. No one could love her like he loved her. He wouldn't trust again. He knew her type. He should have seen this coming. She would always be this way. She liked the excitement of falling in love. She could never be faithful. It would be her life to move from one poor fellow to the next. There were thousands like her and thousands like who she thought she loved but what she didn't know was that she actually loved him – her boyfriend. *Remember?* He never would have left her.

He said, "Come home. Please?"

He had pulled his hair out trying to make her happy. It was all he'd wanted to do. He knew the little girl that lived inside of her, he knew what was best for her and he wanted to take care of her. Maybe her father had made her this way – weak, disloyal and seeking validation. He said he wanted to affect her, right then, to hurt her in return but he felt like she had no heart. She was disgusting to him now and she would always be. She ruined him and he would never take her back.

Isabella believed the threat. He was assuring her that there would be no second chance. And she knew that now was the time to have second thoughts. She was open to them but they didn't come. Nor did the tears she'd expected. As the sidewalk crumbled into gravel and then dirt she knew she was nearing the end, so she slowed. She listened to every word that he spoke, receiving the punches and feeling deserving of their injury. She participated in his reminiscences and would have let herself be taken anywhere with him had there been anywhere else to go, but there must no longer be – she found herself surprisingly removed, and him already so far away.

She was leaving three years of work, play and reliance – a partner she knew she could cook with, sleep soundly beside and count on to pull her into his arms at the moments when she least wanted and most needed to be held. All of the things about Benjamin that she simply didn't know could therefore so easily go awry, immediately then she'd be left alone, with less, and all for a weekend of enchantment by that intensity of taboo. Considering that she might have just completely lost her mind for three days, she was pricked by the barb of possible failure on the thin wire of fortune. Perched there, she was also at the eye of the storm of solitude and self-sufficiency – alone with the responsibility of the consequences of that capacity, were it in her to depart rationale, wooed by weather and song. All of this newness though, it was good. She could feel herself growing bigger, stronger, outward already, gathering her new wings up around her, preparing for flight.

Her boyfriend said that he had wanted to propose to her, to keep her from being swayed by the pretty people she would surely meet. This was the ultimate entreaty. Its offer exposed his youth and revealed his misunderstanding of her less today than tomorrow.

"What can this guy give you that I can't?"

She couldn't answer.

He called her pathetic. He called her a slut. And then he softened. "What about last weekend? When we were together – how was that?"

She told him the truth: "It was the happiest I've ever been with you." She winced, the amputation became even more sudden for them both. Some tears arrived then but they almost felt forced because she knew that this was the right decision. *At least the anxiety is gone*. Realizing this, she cried for real. One can exist in simple contentedness for so long and not notice the barnacles collecting. Being rid of them felt like bittersweet sea water on the raw spot.

He said they grew together and they didn't grow apart. She agreed, and also couldn't imagine growing any more with him. She felt terrified of tomorrow without him.

Isabella ended her walk at the marina where silent boats bobbed around her, clambering to catch a glimpse of this girl. What had she done? What would she do next? A mast and tipped, peeking out from behind a pier. She was weary, but yes here, going somewhere.

That night Benjamin and Isabella were back in the dark, in the blankets, in the candlelight. They started whispering about what it was like. What it would be called – how to describe the feeling. They danced and flitted around it, taunting each other with what exactly they might be referring to but being too afraid to say it. Or so she thought until he grabbed her face and said, "Fuck it, I love you. I think you're amazing."

She felt it in her whole body and the enormity of their encounter raced up behind her with the heavy momentum of a sooty train. Later, she found out that the day she had met his parents, which was only the day after they'd really met each other, Benjamin had told them: "Mom, Dad, I'm going to fall in love with this girl."

And, she found out that when she and Benjamin had kissed later that same night – when her eyes were closed and his were not, and his lips were at her neck – he'd mouthed to her that he loved her. He'd spoken it without breath to carry it to her ears, knowing already.

She said. "I love you too."

W hat they did next was bought wine. They bought red sitting at a table on the street in the late evening outside of a bar that was glowing red inside. It pulsed beside them like a hot heartbeat in the center of a lolling city that reclined in the hour and the season. They held trembling hands only letting go to allow the waiter to fill their glasses – clear crystal invisible in the dark but for the occasional glints of captured light that they swallowed with the relieving syrah. In the corner of the sky, a big moon hung odd and cocked like the loony eye of a voyeur. Freckled around it were winking stars. Every so often one would go sliding down the dome of night.

They bought white to accompany their rosemary bread and brie and crab, whole and uncleaned that they took to the waterfront in soggy butcher paper on the one-week anniversary of their first date. A pale sunset was quietly leaving when they arrived and they took the beach from it, passing through a veil of departing day into an expanse of silver, the inside of a cloud, one of her dreams. The air was bright but the sand matte, everything illuminated but flat, a set without its paint.

In tribute to the week before, they used a screwdriver to open the wine and they drank it from the bottle. Benjamin unwrapped a crab body, turned it belly-up and broke it in half. The brittle shell sucked and popped, dribbling water down his wrists. With a half in each hand, the sections' limbs and claws dangling between his fingers, he padded down the shore to the water. She watched his heels lift out of prints in the sand, his ankles as the water rippled out from around them, the rolled hems of his pants as they dampened. He bent and dipped the crab-halves into the sea. Bubbles and grey spongy innards bobbed to the surface, drifting away softly.

She swallowed smiling tears as he jogged back to her, slowing as he neared, eyes never leaving her face and letting her know that he noticed by not saying a word – rather showing her how to clean the crab. She watched even though she already knew how, letting it be a distraction from the fact that she felt like one of the half-bodies in his hands. But safe there in the deft fingers and soft palm. He used his teeth to dissect the legs, spiting shell off of his tongue and delicately removing the largest, sweetest meat bites, which he handed over for her to eat. When she couldn't hold any more of the pillowy flesh, he fed her. She licked the salt and the sweet from his fingertips and then tried to kiss him in thanks but he was already back to working out her next bite. With a full mouth she felt cared for and so very happy. Her quick heart slowed as the dark closed them in, providing respite. All they had to do now was get to know each other.

They built a fire and smoked bits of bread over it, melting the cheese atop and the smiling as the smoothness filled their mouths. They were glad to be successfully making good. Soon enough, and grits of sand ignored they let go of their supplies and had hands in each others' hair, were kissing, were holding faces and trying so hard to see deeper into the other's eyes. *Who are you? Where did you come from? Why do I already know, want, love you so intensely? What is this? Is there a catch? How is it that you feel the same way I do?*

They reveled in this mutuality and then they pushed back – either one of them; they both did it – and demanded: *What are you thinking? What are you feeling? Really. Tell me now.* Every response was the right one and their respective walls would lose another brick – chip down another row, eroded by waves of consistency.

It was terrifying because it was so wonderful. She thought no one could really be this much: this equal and this grand, this new and familiar, challenging and easy. Not possible and yet, it was happening. In order to secure this momentum, they made a pact: they would always go Black speed. They would require and provide head and heart with immediacy. There wasn't enough time for politeness. There was no room for flattery. They would barrel through roadblocks together, only moving forward. It was all or nothing. Full speed ahead, unless or until.

In the mornings they awoke to a symphony of alarm clocks – his, hers and the one they set together just in case. A comical, hectic sample of the two separate lives now intertwined like their limbs, a confused tangle revealed in parts by the unsullied light of morning.

Their minds too were enmeshed; they began to dream about each other. Under heavy sheets of seduction they spent the whole night adventuring together in deserts or childhoods or at the bottom of the ocean. Until, like a bandit that crisp reality stole into their reverie, appearing from around a corner bringing dreams into day and each other into each others' dreams.

They'd delay a ring to rise and sneak back to bed together just as another would sound and he'd ask her in a whisper if they could just spoon for ten more minutes. She always said yes, of course; nothing else was more important. More time, they were always in pursuit of more time.

She lay on her side, watching the busying street through the window across the room. Footsteps marched across the ceiling in the apartment above and her thighs burned to run. He pushed her hair up clumsily – moving it off the back of her neck so he could put his face there. She waited, letting him and feeling his breath slow and deepen. Her nerves did not match the sedate room. They sought sounds in the silence and motion where there was none. When Benjamin had returned to resting she took the hand that he'd placed on her waist and spread it flatly across the center of her chest, hoping to press his calm into herself. There was not an inch of space between them. He was heavy and she was light, her limbs flooded with air. They tingled to move but she held them still, knowing that it was good to make them stay

– to feel this contest. She was stronger than they though who knew best may yet be decided. The temperature was right if hot, the scent was right if heady, the fit was right if a bit too tight. She shut her eyes, closed out the morning and fell back into the sleep with him.

They made love for hours. To music, to silence, in the car, on the beach and eventually in the middle of the night, not knowing how it started but too caught up to care. Asleep really, and delirious they'd find themselves fumbling and aching, inhaling and consuming each other. The scent perhaps provoked it. They made something so chemical – metal, honey and musk from the nearness of their hot skin. Grabbing at and sticky with sweat, equal in strength of yearn and hunger their bodies belonged to either or neither and were anyway merely a means to the sating end – the famine from the center and the fare oh so close.

Eyes never opening and minds amid dreams they stretched between worlds. Reaching out across consciousness their hands sought with intention and without courtesy: let me take, take from me, taut until we splinter like crags shedding sheets of stone gathering speed as we slide, echo, crash into rubble.

We are having sex, she realizes. *I was asleep and I nearly am still but,* it ends and colors wash behind her eyelids – sprigs of heather and waves of slate. They began to compare these visions. *What did you see?* They are often the same scenes of brutalist light and shadows, postmodern lines and shapes.

Dampening the mattress, losing their breaths in the pillows, wrists falling limp between thighs – whose unknown – they open lips to start a whispered something, a "thank you" an "I love you" or just a "you" but sleep resurges overwhelmingly having only abated for the interlude. It returns rapidly, closing around them like the clap of cymbals and the incident concludes in an eclipse of negative space.

They woke up to the sunrise and often wondered: *Did we?*

When they danced, it was like hero and heroine, escapees, children. They filled the spaces that others' left, playing games and acting out roles. He spun and dipped her with a strong arm at the small of her back. He tugged her into twirls that landed her pressed up against him for a breathless second before being tossed back away. She skip-skirted off to dance alone, across the room where she could pretend to catch his eye for the very first time. He feigned apathy for a minute but not longer before slithering back to her. He tugged at the strap of her dress and she offered him the back of her neck.

They sought reassurance in the other's face – that the game was still good and that yes, they were still in it together. Of course they were. The whole thing was only a toying with disinterest in a mock freedom from want. *How funny.* They laughed. Oh and yet this was actually quite serious business. This was love. She grabbed his shoulders and he grabbed her face. They kissed, hard, with eyes clenched closed, smiles and frowns fighting at the mouths that they kept pressed together to stave off either, everything. Bodies rigid, hearts pushing pushing out, her on tiptoe atop his feet and he pulling her up. Between them, at their skin, where they met was all the grip that a person might be made of but unable to exert. They equaled more. Like a punch and an exclamation point and a bite and a bellow.

T hey spent her birthday at The River, as it was simply called. A popular place for couples seeking nearby refuge from the city, its access was little more than a gravel turnoff from the state's main, eastern heading highway. A short hike along a shaded trail spongy and carpeted by sap-stuck pine needles led directly to the water, sparkling between two blond banks. Otherwise unmarked, the number on the mile post preceding its entrance was shared by word-of-mouth among friends and the occasional stranger sized up before approved for entrustment with the sacred locale. Thereby, it developed into a "spot", though rarely were more than a handful of people there at any given time, and then all from

113

related social circles. Pairs decorated driftwood, spaced beyond hearing distance of each other and focused on their conversations and canned beer rather than seeing or being seen. They spoke with faces aimed at each other, their shorts were dusty canvas and their torsos and shoulders were not tanned.

Benjamin and Isabella brought only a shared backpack carrying a bottle of wine and a couple of towels. They picked their way up the bleached sand away from anyone and selected a clearing of fine silt protected by a line of breast-high willows. They lay on their backs in some shade and watched clouds sieve through the tresses of the willows.

When the sweat beads became too heavy to remain on their shoulders and went careening along their collarbones, the lovers waded into the river holding hands and slipping over the rocks together, ankles bitten by the cold. Gasping but not pausing, they sank up to their armpits, shivering. The cold felt like fear. Physical threatened to overwhelm psychological; nature is greater than man. Benjamin told her to swim, so Isabella did – letting the land drift out from under her feet, she lifted off into the rushing lane and was swept sideways, the current dragging at her legs. She kicked against it, making little progress and worrying that it would overpower her. She swam harder, determined. He was several yards in front of her, closer to the other shore; she could make it. Suddenly the turmoil ceased and the water around her was still and warm, gurgling innocently. Floating up beside her, Benjamin smiled and said, "See?"

An invisible line divided the river lengthwise like a highway. Half of it ran mean and icy; the other ambled and loitered around the reeds. With it, the first fall leaves floated in spirals downstream around the corner, and out of sight. Benjamin and Isabella swam to where their toes grazed the clay, climbed up into the shallow, re-clasped hands and kissed – the water splashing up between their chests and chins.

Returning to their towels, they stretched out on their stomachs and talked about their art. He wanted to know more about her writing. She picked up a handful of pebbles and tossed them out as she spoke. They hit the sand with soft thuds, like periods at the end of her sentences. "It's a catharsis." *Thud.* "I've always written." *Thud.* I don't know what I'm doing, or if any of it is very good, but I have to do it, otherwise I'm not really living." *Thud.*

He didn't seem to hear her last sentence, excited about the subject and having found a sympathizer in the woes and reward of the creative process. Their mediums were different but their devotion to the uncountable hours of unrecognized work was equal. He pressed on. Did she feel "the flux"? The compulsion to compose that might rise in an afternoon and last for a day, a week or a season? Yes, she did. Was he always aware of from where he was bestirred to write? No, he was not. It was like mining for diamonds, he said. Or channeling, she said. Could they agree that the blank page was not daunting and that day was not long enough to pump dry the well of inspiration? Yes, they could.

She'd never shared a finished piece though. Benjamin had. He would encourage her. Arranging larger rocks into a row at their feet, he explained that each one represented a single, completed work. A song, a sentence or a story for example. Once finished, which was often the hardest part – the polishing requiring endless patience and testing one's commitment to craft – the piece would sit next in line with the others, a spine on the shelf. The collection of the works became a catalog, cohesive, representative and alive on its own. *Content is king,* he told the sky. She thought: *To be anything is to do it.*

He asked her to read to him again, and she did, opening her notebook to a page not more than a week old:

"His fingers play the heart's bass breath beats on my knee. There's symmetry in the bars and in the sporadic clouds that separate us and them. Music flies out open windows into the hot air wake at our backs, breaking and dropping parts along broken highway lines. Brown field grass blows below a bright sky through which we quickly Black speed drive to an end. Outrunning the notes we leave behind.

A throbbing vehicle drifts, traveling over hills through shadows and sun and seconds. Shattering and passing unaffected it is racing doubt and erasing the past that causes walls and locks and closed-door hiding places for the softest parts penetrable.

He drives as fast as rebellion requires, swerving under the wind, avoiding, free and fleeing, to and from place. Intoxication makes the sights sounds. Time is beyond bug-stuck glass and late like under water. Two people protected bear hearts, safe in the floating voice that permeates ears and air. Sidelong weeds are lapsing scenery – prettily painted and passing, a benign background to observe but not to affect. Speed makes it safe. There will be no stopping because we're outpacing fear. Slowing is not allowed. This is sharing; this is showing.

Black rubber tire ruins on the road will remember."

Benjamin said, "You're a writer." Grinning and taking a rock from her hand he said, "You're a writer because you *write*." *Thud.*

He settled onto his back, into the idea. She joined him, resting her head on his chest, relieved to be embraced after vulnerability and aroused that this might be true. If she agreed, it would also be a commitment to the profession. Emboldened by their momentum, she seized the silent second else it pass.

"I suppose then," she said, "Yes. I am a writer."

The two relaxed in a satisfaction that they'd made it to together. It seemed that some catastrophe had been narrowly averted, though what loomed already was an end – a season's change, the movement's finale, a crest, the crescendo. They wrapped their fingers together and were still on the warmth that rose through the rocks. The frigid water rushed along quietly a few yards away and the hot wind carried only calm. They breathed together and from above their thoughts revolved like the leaves in the river, traveling downstream around the corner and out of sight. Today at least, they would not see around that bend.

"There is a bridge upriver." Benjamin said. "We have to jump off of it."

So they rose into the heat and trekked up the plains of pebbles with drowsy legs. Rounding a crook, the steel skeleton hunched imposingly above them. Part plant, part creature it wore time in shingles of blistering turquoise rust, regalia of graffiti and Creosote scars. It sat in the sky, wise, silent and warped – hollow-eyed but maybe alive deep at some glowing amber center. Its stillness was suspicious, like a shout or sudden move would cause it to wake and rise, shaking loose its foundation and marching over them toward the city.

Benjamin and Isabella stripped back down to their swimsuits and climbed gingerly up the rungs of a hind leg. At the top, a gang of boys were taunting each other skittishly to jump. *Jump! Sissy! What are you afraid of?* Their voices were tight and high, catching with nervousness that they covered with combativeness. They yelled at their echoes and shoved one another nearer the edge though never pushing too hard, not wanting to authorize the result.

Benjamin and Isabella walked a plank out over the river. It felt like she was striding on air. Wind curled up off of the water lifting the hair off the back of her neck, blowing up under her chin and crossing beneath her feet, touching places it didn't usually.

The water below was a dark mirror. Stretched out, it flaunted its length and depth, looking unfamiliar. The bridge was much, much higher then she'd thought. Leaves that another pair of lovers would see as she had earlier were tiny. Her pulse fluttered and she pulled back on Benjamin's hand some, slowing but still going.

They ducked through the trusses, a single bar separating them from open air. With their backs to the flaking metal, they inched along the outermost ledge, shards slipping off and twirling out of sight. The land to either side shrank. They were between directions, the bridge hinging east and west.

At the very middle, they stepped over the thin rail, hooking their elbows over it and leaning out over the water. She could feel the height in her chest. That there was nothing nothing between her and the fall made her toes tingle and her head light.

Benjamin told her that he would go first to make sure it was safe. He would dive and then she could jump. She didn't want him to dive. She imagined the tragedy of living having lost a love so young. He bent his knees, pushed off and fell headfirst, beautifully. She watched his arc, thinking of the air sweeping along his spine. There was no sound for a second, two, three as he plummeted. She was frozen. His feet disappeared into the water that closed around him with the swish of a velvet cape.

Whoops from the boys rose up around Isabella. Delighted by this show of bravery they hip-hoorayed, crawling over each other to see if he had perished and high-fiving because he had not. Remembering the girl beside them, they grew quiet and turned to her, looking concerned. The distance before her seemed to have doubled.

Benjamin smiled up at her and called that now it was her turn. Her legs shook (she didn't know that this actually happened). She felt like if she stood there any longer she would faint so she let go of the railing and balanced on the narrow grate. The river writhed. The bridge seemed about to shudder and she knew it was time to go so she, stepped, off.

Her heart remained behind and she squeezed shut her eyes but could see the surface rushing at her heels like a wall. She anticipated the impact but it didn't come and her belly cried out because she was still falling. And then the water crashed around her, engulfing her in a silence cooler and darker as she descended through the layers of deepening shades of indigo. She stretched out through the new temperatures, lengthening in the depths and letting the current twist her. She was tempted to inhale. She spread her legs to feel the water against her thighs and shook her head to color her curls with the blues. Reveling in having leapt and in the sinking, she felt satisfied and hungry, burning like her lungs. She could come to need this. She could see it – a fiery addiction that may begin as shared but could never end as such.

Finding the sunlight crinkling above she swam to it quickly and burst through the surface with a swear and a hoot for the boys, her throat hoarse and adrenaline cavorting in her veins.

As Benjamin and Isabella slipped back up the muddy bank together, she admitted to having been very afraid; she'd never jumped from something that tremendous before. Benjamin just winked. He knew.

She hadn't but now she did so the next time would be different.

N ot the first time, that was neither the last that they were flying or falling together, nor that she was afraid of jumping. A few days later, they visited the fair. Wandering through plastic and dilapidation, between billowing rows of greases and puffs of powdered sugar and watching oddly proportioned people they cared less for being there than for being together. They sought nothing, receptive to vendors' summons and the flow of waddling parents and zigzagging children with knocking balloons. Near dusk, the path dead-ended at the base of a monstrous roller coaster. It was cruelly high. Stacks of white wooden trusses like those of their bridge latticed into a skyscraping peak, the top of which Isabella could not see. The base creaked and from somewhere in the heavens people screamed. It looked extraterrestrial and designed to induce terror.

Benjamin nudged her toward it and she trusted that he knew better; she would not put herself under the control of this torture device. She knelt to tie her shoe and he jogged off to buy cotton candy but returned with tickets to the ride instead. She tried to drag him away, laughing but serious. *No way in hell,* she said. She couldn't, she would not … She was afraid like a kid is afraid – it didn't matter why; it was simply too scary.

Benjamin just smiled at her and told her that she was so brave and she felt the rush of the flight from the bridge and in they were strapped. A metal talon locked between her thighs. Black leather pads pinned her shoulders against the seat. Their legs were left dangling and as their seats jerked and clicked into the sky Isabella pictured the flopping limbs of the crabs in Benjamin's hands at the beach. She realized that thanks to him, she had witnessed new atmospheres. Feet first down into the cool depths of the darkening river and headfirst now, up through the ever lightening tiers of blue, her universe expanded.

When they were perched above the county, the fairground a kiddie pool below and a different wind blowing around them, her body began to quake. She giggled and thought she might die. He grabbed her hand. She realized that they had left behind sound. He said,

"It feels like it's just us up here doesn't it?"

Isabella nodded. She wanted to enjoy the view but she was bracing for the drop.

"I love you Bella." He said.

The horizon lurched perilously. They were free-falling backward to the ground, feet in the clouds and blood in their foreheads. Saved at the last second! Scooped up and rocketed into weightlessness they paused and then went plunging toward the planet again, the pressure against her chest immense. *This, is Black speed.* Isabella tried to keep her eyes on the pavement where she was sure they would splatter. Being shot face-first at the parking lot maddened her and she was angry at the contraption for wielding her mortality like a carrot on a stick. Sure enough, they were spared from disaster again, the ground sailing beneath her as they were thrown back up into the azure. *Ha ha, fun funny.* With mania she loved and hated it equally. When the jaws released, she tumbled off. Exhilarated and capable of ever more having survived, she buzzed with a new fury stirred not sated.

I t was immediately after that ride that they first ran off to her family's lakefront cabin on the other side of the state. On a whim they walked straight out of the fair, drove straight out of the city and disappeared into the mountains. Spit out like a pinball on the other side of the hills, they whizzed across the countryside that flattened and stretched out beneath their wheels. The air sweetened with increasingly parched fields and yellowing grasses. As their distance from reality grew, they were pacified.

Isabella observed that when traveling in a car, it feels as though we are actually stationary while the world revolves around us. The panorama passes quickest closest and gradually farthest away. Slowly,

slowly ever so the pines rotate in place as we wend, showing us their every side. The hills open up ahead and close off behind. We are the axis, a pinnacle, the pole of a spinning top. Despite our trajectory we remain at the center of a bowl as big as sight. It moves with us; peaks remain beyond the perimeter. We proceed like: through a stone ballet, dancers en pointe, skirts whirled in the grand pirouette.

When the shadows were longest, they began to feel what it was they were trying to outrun. Still they drove, not stopping even when they arrived to the house – skipping from the car, shedding clothes as they streaked and dived into the lake.

And when the land was curtained with evening, they made mojitos. The wind carried away the top layer of her cupped handful of crushed mint leaves as if they belonged to it and not to her – intended to travel among the changing season's migration of foliage and quail through the orchards. Isabella knelt at a glass table in the silvery twilight, squeezing sweet limes and sifting white sugar into one of her grandfather's clear glass jugs. A bottle of soda water, shaken and heated in the sun exploded onto her. That was how she had felt. She aimed the second at Benjamin, spraying him with the hot mist.

The following morning, before coffee, she found herself in a familiar position: gripping the deck railing high above the sparkling lake, he smiling up at her from below, urging her to *Jump!* She did. She did and then she sprinted back up the steps and did it again – hurtling herself off without hesitation. And then again. And again. Over and over and over. Each time as frightened as the first, she ran this circuit with a wail in her throat and ire in her skin. She ascended and leapt until she had nothing left – prostrate in the oscillation between defeat and invincibility. She could do anything; she would do everything. With or without Benjamin. Isabella commandeered this power and stored it in her bones, preparing.

When they'd had enough, the two dried in fluffy cotton towels. Cheeks flushed and cores cooled they wrapped in each other and napped. The hours thereafter passed as a lucid dream. Hidden from the outside, from the future, from anything but each other, they played until collapsing in laughter and then quieting to spend hours murmuring through each other's minds.

Only after the moon saw them make love beside the lake did the spell wear off. They made it all the way to the final night of the weekend before the thing got into the house. It slid under the bedroom door, snaked around her waist and soaked straight into her chest – her heart – and his heart. Their tinkling laughter echoed off of the hills while they lay with their heads on the pillows looking up at the ceiling, tears streaming down their faces.

She cried because the love hurt. And because though they'd just met, it was already so big. And because it wouldn't last, though it was looking like it very well could. Nothing was wrong but a thousand things could be and eventually they would be. She didn't trust him and she didn't trust herself, though that wasn't stopping anything. She didn't want to be the naïve one. And so maybe it was that she didn't want to trust him. She thought she couldn't believe yet she couldn't deny what she was immersed in but then she couldn't trust that she wouldn't feel differently tomorrow. She was fighting with herself. She didn't want to let go like she already had and let him in and be this vulnerable and let him see her as well as he already did.

It was like her soul loved him. And she hated it, something, whatever there was to hate, because it was going to hurt worse. The best beauty that life bestows, it does so abusively. That white-hot blinding type – it leaves a scar.

The affront was on its way and she'd have liked to have it before her now to fight. She hated it and loved it as well for fooling her – for capturing her and setting her a flight so many times over in a day.

She knew that he couldn't be as strong as he claimed, nor she as strong as she wished. She didn't like waking up to find herself submerged. Because they were both human, they would harm each other. Someone would trip. And she hated that.

They talked and they talked and they talked. They held each other and battled against themselves, pulling it out of each other, exhausting and finding it at the end – among the stripped nerves that can be nothing but sincere. At the rawest edge, the bottom scraped, in the middle of the night, in front of family and friends, or guards-down-drunk, mid-stride, one would turn and ask a question like a blow to the soft belly and ever the other showed their self consistent.

They put their faces together and let their tears mix. They pushed away from each other – backs turned on opposite sides of the bed to imagine what it'd feel like to be alone. And they cried, sobbed, just ached and caved in on themselves. They fell asleep in each others' arms in a humid room and they went home the next day.

A letter:
Hello Benjamin,

To you, my introduction to stability. To you, who I can trust. To you who holds my hand in his with warmth and strength that are love and ability. Which means for me a hand and a heart in a man who I know can hold me (who I know can be so hard to hold sometimes) but I will let you.

Ah, to you who's inspired me so much. You who showed me a new future by showing me you. Like we each held half of a panoramic picture. And now we have a whole and more we have all of the good of whole hearts too. Alonely capable of conquering the world and individually capable of sharing all of ourselves with each other only because we did it together and what (what?) won't we do together now?

I'm giving you more penmanship here today. I'm giving you writing in one of my handwritings. The one where I control the words and how you read them and what rises in your mind with only these little black letters on this white page. Would you like to see a silver dusk light set on sand at the beach? Would you like to see two lovers, naked and glowing in the fire that's charring hollow crab shells glowing red, hot grey? Would you rather see them sitting on a sidewalk at night, dry and bundled in matching black coats – barefoot and chewing pink bubblegum – lazy and lackadaisically remembering their memories? How long has it been again? When will it have been one month, I wonder? I wonder. (It will turn out that that was their one month anniversary.) You could see them yesterday, hiding under the covers, wrapped in each others' arms, pressing their faces together, hiding their eyes, falling asleep without letting go. Or you could see them sitting civilly over spring rolls in the diner with mirror-walls instead of windows.

Drinking tomato soup that makes them sleepy. Stopping for freshly baked cookies on the way back to bed or maybe,

Maybe they are laughing in the streets at night after having danced and smiled and gotten drunk on anticipation and lavender martinis. Or maybe it all runs together and they're seeing the Northern Lights and the sunrise at the same time. Maybe they're driving and maybe they're dreaming and maybe they're on their first date or their best date or the date that happens tomorrow or ten years from now.

Maybe and surely and yes to all of these memories and most definitely their eyes never left each other and their hands never let go because they were rapt.

And are rapt.

This is what I give you to see tonight. Tomorrow you will see this too and you will remember what else you've seen and you will see more. To yesterday and to today and to tomorrow.

They were drunk in a diner drinking coffee and eating waffles with maple syrup at four-thirty in the morning when she told him that she imagined it'd be nice to be married to him. They were waiting at the bus stop, sharing sparkling water and hot honeyed nuts from a street vendor when he said that he imagined he'd like being married to her too. They were sipping white wine and fingering olives at a café in an alley with the wind whipping the awning overhead when they talked some, just a little, about what they had or had not said, exactly. Benjamin told her that they'd have the conversation when the time was right. And that when they had it, it would be a short one. His voice wavered and there were tears in his eyes that he blinked past and made a smile through in order to hold hers and say, "Okay?"

She nodded and mouthed, "Okay."

After he met her family for the second time, Isabella's mother said that the family approved. How had she ever found him? Then, Benjamin and Isabella became her mother's measure for true love. They gave her hope, she said. Their passion renewed her belief in the prospect of a successful partnership despite her lifetime of experience. Mother sat beside Grandmother and the two beamed over folded hands at Isabella, their roles gratified by their little girl's functionality in a relationship with a man whom everyone found so utterly charming.

Grandmother said, "I've never seen you so happy."

Isabella's father said, "He's got a great laugh, kiddo." Later he conceded that maybe, though she was young of course, it might be time to start considering relationships that are serious enough to, you know, last a long time. He hadn't found it, but maybe she could. It would make a father very proud.

Benjamin's parents maintained their own embrace while smiling knowingly and carrying a roomy ownership of their son's half of the success. They seemed to have seen this kind of love and were encouraging through the young lovers' eagerness. When Benjamin and Isabella visited, it was as if the company of another couple as in love as they were was fun. His grandmother eyed Isabella with command until eventually via a private nod Isabella knew that she was received.

Often later Benjamin and Isabella referred to what their children would be like. It was a game and a test and a fantasy; they were still playing.

They went back to the lake house once more and they were met with signs of lateness, subtle and insistent. It rained in the evening, settling the dust and condensing the scent of Russian sage to an acridity that threatened to tarnish their utopian purpose. The boughs of the willow hung lower, the windchime rang insistently and the crickets' chirps – Benjamin and Isabella realized not until the final night – had slowed. They saw the discomfort in each others' eyes. Change encroached and now would soon be memories. Memories made in different air, under distanced sun and for how long would it be possible to preserve them? Recollection is so subjective and fleeting. How do we ensure that today is not lost?

They drove faster and jumped into the cooling water sooner. They climbed into the hills with more urgency and made themselves see the view that they'd stumbled upon the first time. They sought something more with every second and they didn't sleep. Their eyes burned as they brought every plan to completion, every conversation to resolution because, *Black speed* they'd say; they didn't have much time left. Before what, they didn't know (do we ever?) but they weren't going to slight any low hanging sense. An end is a beginning.

On the last day, as the evening approached the cliffs, necessitating their departure, they resisted, denied – bags packed but ignored. For the sake of tomorrow, for the sake of suffering, to resurrect a whim and to steal life for the aggregate they dove into the lake and swam out toward the setting sun. They swam farther than ever before and then, treading water they clasped hands and faced west as the pale yellow fell behind the land's shoulder. Benjamin and Isabella willed it more beautiful and it was. They wished it to linger longer and it did. They called out *Goodbye sun! Goodbye summer! Goodbye escape.* Still holding hands, awkward with feet colliding beneath the surface and waves splashing onto their cheeks, mixing with their tears, they kissed. Laughed. Cried. Kissed! Watched in order to recall. Licked lips in order to imbibe. Said again: *Goodbye!* And together still. *Goodbye ... hello.*

And then they were driving. Alone on a vacant highway broken lines became single under the black car traveling like a compression wave across the crust of dusk, buckling the asphalt behind them. They crested a hill and the city reared up on the horizon, its suck immediate and immense. They recoiled from it, their mouths souring. The song from the speakers ascended and the toothed skyline sneered, beckoning. It said, *You have not left*. It said, *You are not safe*. It said, *Wake up from your dream. Here is where you will.*

Benjamin readjusted his grip on the steering wheel and they coasted across the summit below which was the world. The menacing mouth gaped, welcoming their return. Isabella tried to push out a breath but it withered on her tongue; she would have liked to spit. Benjamin pressed his lips together and looked at her. *Ready?* The music cracked and poured onto her like confetti. She wanted to throw it off; it hurt her skin, she could barely keep from sobbing. *Ready.* That had been the crescendo, and now they knew. He accelerated into the descent. They catapulted down the slope like the plummet finale of a roller coaster, the freefall of a dive. She let open her chest, the Black speed shooting through her. She squared her chin and tears slid down her cheeks despite her every protest.

Benjamin's face was also wet; he was as afraid as she. They seized each others' hands and squeezed until it hurt. The air crystallized; their tears dissolved, leaving eyes wide and dry and back in and down they plunged into the city that swallowed them whole.

W hat might have happened:

Just like in the beginning, Benjamin and Isabella continued to get coffee together every morning. They walked into the café where they'd met, ordered the usual and chatted with the barista who was now nearly part of the relationship. Isabella had gone from protecting her name to sharing family recipes.

Then, hand-in-hand, the pair pushed out into the day, two as one. For the first few months, he dropped her off at the university before driving to his shiny new job outside of the city. When she graduated, he put in a good word for her, which landed her a job and then they commuted to and from the office together. In the evenings they went jogging, cooked dinner for each other and watched one television show a week. Their possessions sat easily beside each other and their back-to-back desks displayed their sidelong pursuits. They decorated and they baked cookies; they tended and shared. He learned her weather-affected moods and she forgave his dirty dishes. He made her laugh every day and she helped him find calm.

On Saturdays they cleaned the apartment. She dusted and he mopped because she didn't like doing the floors. On Sundays they walked to the market for crumpets and fresh produce, stopping at the newsstand on the corner to buy a fashion magazine for her and a music paper for him. They held hands wherever they went, and as they fell asleep. They wrapped each other in embraces of gratitude for having met, for the other's willingness to step off, and for the protective sky that seemed to have enabled all of this. That third element, external or intrinsic to their combination had pushed them together and seemed to deserve the thanks, really, if anything did. Isabella would have been grateful for everything had it been short-lived, as she assumed any honeymoon would be, but it was not. She and Benjamin spoke to each other with increasing kindness and rather than lessening, their connection grew – blossoming naturally, spreading its roots through the ground and then winding up around them like ivy to spires.

The two worked tirelessly in a single room with a view of the sea and the incoming storms. For hours they'd compose in silence and then rest to step outside and watch the seagulls bathe in a rainwater puddle on the building-top below them. Entire weekends often passed this way: creating. She became comfortable falling asleep to the sounds of his fingers flying over buttons and keys – clicking and sliding, throwing knobs and faders as he played. A corner of their apartment was dedicated to his equipment: A keyboard, speakers and stacks of machines that made a solid surface of buttons and switches that blinked and quivered all day and all night for years, never needing to be turned off. She became familiar even with the seventh fader, which was likely possessed – disturbed by dust and prone to jumps in the middle of the afternoon when no one was near. She learned which notes corresponded to which columns of light on the monitors and he learned the voice with which she wrote – editing her stories while she paced the kitchen, reading along with him in her mind. At the end of a day-long session they might share their works with each other, or they might prefer to put them away and simply drink wine.

And, drink wine they did. They saved corks in a vase on the kitchen counter until it overflowed. They moved the collection to a drawer until it wouldn't close and then they filled a glass case with their favorites and hung it on the wall. They traveled the world through the varieties, sitting on their sea-facing balcony with the city behind them, sipping and talking night after night after night. Never tiring of each other's company or the conversation, they spent years preferring evenings at home to anything else. Buying only one bottle with good intentions, they often ran for another before the corner-store closed – the evening young and discussion forever fruitful. The cashier would give a knowing nod and anticipate their request for also some dolmades to go.

A couple of times they hosted parties, filling the apartment with friends and bruschetta and a case of cabernet but more often they celebrated occasions alone. On their first Christmas, Isabella surprised him with a tree – a tilted plastic thing that she assembled in diligent silence while fretting about his snowy drive home. She arranged the gifts, straightened the ornaments and adjusted the volume of the Edith Piaf record just so. Then she sat cross-legged on the carpet in complete contentment. The view through their western-facing windows was wider than any she'd owned. She reveled in having arrived at some tier of life. She stood on a level, a step, a plane – she was not climbing and she was no longer winded from the race. She could breathe and appreciate the vista; the stillness was settling.

Benjamin and Isabella – they had a morning routine and a life plan.

They may never know what they missed nor miss what they never knew.

W hich is why this is what actually happened:

Just like in the beginning, Benjamin and Isabella were back in his bed, buried beneath those soft blankets of escape. They were lying on their sides facing each other with their hands gripped at their hearts – tugging and squeezing to punctuate the gravity of their whispers. The subjects were the same as always: love, potential and the greatness of them. This time though, Isabella was full of a churning sadness. It started like the swirling wind that she'd followed here to begin with. The one that had grown into a tornado, lifting and separating her, spinning and weaving until she was whole and complete – setting her down anew in a blooming field with fresh eyes and full wings. She started to cry silently and then became angry; she was tired of crying.

"What?" Benjamin asked urgently, gently. "What's wrong Bella?" He put his hand on her cheek, feeling the wetness, "Oh."

She clenched closed her eyes and rolled onto her back. She made herself straight and stiff in resistance like a corpse, dead to this. Inside her started a rocking bath of hot water. It swayed and burned back and forth from one porcelain rim to another. Gathering strength, the waves grew, splashing over onto the floor, water streaming out from under the bed, creeping up the corners of the sheets. The damp cotton clung to her skin.

She saw herself in the future, remembering this with endearment but not wondering what might have been. She would sympathize with today. She would know herself well by then and she would accept what was about to be done. She simply wasn't meant for this – for the happily-ever-after. She knew that she would have lots of loves but that she would ultimately be her greatest own. She would abide with deep aloneness and acceptable happiness. It had always been that way – the insatiability was impetus.

Prepared, she looked at Benjamin. His eyes widened and he smiled so kindly at her – full of a love that didn't waver. He had closed off all doors of distraction; it was all for her, if only she wanted it.

She was sorry to see his softness the way she'd seen others' softness. His love became one in a line. She let go of her affection for his vulnerability and a tough disdain replaced it like a brick back into the wall. She released her gratitude for his devotion and condescension unfolded.

Is it that we would rather be removed than the victim? Do we prefer to be wanting? Are we dissatisfied by satisfaction? If there is no tension, are we settling?

Isabella turned to the window across the room and all of the passersby seemed to be running now. She squirmed madly, feeling feverish.

"Hey," Benjamin said.

She wanted to scream at him to make her shut up and love him the way she should. She wished he could steal her peripheral vision, cause her to go blind, say *sure!* But, she lost to herself.

"Hey" he said it more sternly. "What are you doing Bella? Look at me. Where are you going? Come back and talk to me, now."

She felt a footing falter and glanced at him. His eyes were locked on her face.

"Black speed, Bella. Don't do this." The Black speed law to share all in real time, to allow for no invasion of doubt, she realized was a testament to bravery but also to insecurity. Trust of codependence. It'd worked so far.

"I don't believe this," she said.

"I know," he said, misunderstanding it as praise at first. "Wait …"

She asked him if this was going to work and she thought, *That's not the point.*

He said it would be okay. He inched closer to her. "We'll be all right. We're different Bella."

She shook her head but she didn't really shake her head.

Her foot slipped and she was down on one knee in the rocks. Rocks. The river. The calm warm bubbled up around her shoulders, under her chin – it pushed into her mouth, shushing. She rolled over toward him knocking a wave over the side of the tub. She was nauseous from the rocking and sweating in the heat.

He grabbed her shoulders. He was trying to hold on, to keep her there and she wished he could but it was too late. From the inside, her body yanked away, wanting itself back. She felt guilty and then not. *It is mine after all.*

There was silence. He waited. She whimpered. He shook her shoulders, "Tell me."

She grabbed river rocks in her fists. She laid down on her belly and put her face on the rough beach, pressing her cheek onto the stones, feeling the grit and the solid strong – finding what she could use to stand back up, what she would walk away on.

"Sweet Bella, come here."

She curled into a ball, pressing her shins against his stomach. *I'm scared.* The thought became a roar. And the river and the bridge were gone; the lake and the scent of sage were fantasies and she was there in the bed with him. He pulled her to him and told her that they could do it. She believed him. He said to remember that he would be strong when she couldn't, and she remembered. He said he loved her and that this had to be it. She was it. They were right. They had to be together. *We could make it together.* A tear rolled down his cheek and she saw into the place he opened in his chest for her. His conviction was beautiful.

And he was right: they could make it together. But, they wouldn't because she wasn't going to let them. Benjamin and Isabella – *we* – would prevail, remaining right there, known as they were that day.

She pushed away from him. He let her go for once neither sure what was next, nor invited to know. He held so much of her in his hands. She wanted it back. No more sharing. She fought the tie between them, untangling herself from it and severing it like an umbilical cord. They were going to bleed.

This is the view from the top. Life is the leap. She was going first this time.

"Bella," he whispered, "I love you so much."

She remained perfectly still in order to consume those words. She let them caress her cheek, she let them press into her memory and she let them be his last. They washed over her, shivering phosphorescence. They rose into a cloud above her brow that then began to rain cool drops onto her eyelashes. She loved him too. She told him and the ache grew.

It had all been so divine. Back and forth the whitecaps were unstoppable now. A wretched squall of thunderheads bore down on them. No more resting. A flash flood ripped through the riverbed, sending the unsuspecting couples scurrying up the banks.

She hurt. Too much. It was time.

Everything fell at once like a levitation spell broken. Isabella's eyes opened in the dark and there was a single sob; it sounded like hers. She wrapped her arms around herself. This was right. She felt tiny. Benjamin reached out and found her elbow, tugging softly but she took it back from him limply. She was shaking and crying and sitting up in the bed and then placing her bare feet on the floor *When did it get so cold?* She kept her back to him and tried to stand, doubling over instead, her fingertips on the wood. *Sand.* Her chest caved and she covered her mouth to quiet a gasp. She bit her knuckles and groped for her pants. Benjamin jerked upright in the bed, realizing.

He started to say her name but his voice caught like it was painful to speak. It hurt her to hear and she cringed but didn't turn around. He asked but she couldn't answer and she pulled on her shirt, smearing tears and sticky wet curls to her cheeks.

He said *No* and then he said it louder, "Bella, no." So desperate. *This is so sad.* She stepped back and glanced at him through stinging salt water. He looked terrified and he tried to move toward her from the bed but it was awkward as if he didn't know how to make his limbs work. He was intent on reaching her but no longer knew how. She steadied herself on the wall and held up a stopping hand.

He said, "What are you doing? Where are you going?" His face crumbled and the sounds of one's inability to bear the immensity of a breaking heart tumbled out of his mouth. He pounded a fist into the sheets. He was going to be alone. He was a child again. They both were. And, should remain so. She was leaving him. Right now. Like this. To force first steps as infants. Children's eyes are widest.

She put on her shoes and took a step away from the bed. Benjamin pulled his knees to his chest, shaking his head. She started away feeling centuries old and as if she'd never breathed. Tears covered her neck and wrists and she tried to wipe them away but there were too many and she might as well be blind and broken in half. Her body was folding – shutting off corridors, retreating into itself and she was retreating too before it failed her. Adrenaline fought the shatter in order to escape a greater. She sought her reserves.

She made it to the door. Her palm was slick on the knob and she knew she could still go back so she paused to see what this might feel like, but nothing came. She'd been here before. She bowed her head and pushed out into the hallway. It spun and twisted, she stumbled and thought she might be sick but it felt all right because it was her own. The door clicked closed behind her and everything was silent – the passageway was a blur. Benjamin and Isabella were left behind. Her tears dried. She touched the paint on the wall with her fingertips. Her heart slowed. *Goodbye ... hello.*

I turned to the glowing EXIT sign at the end of the hall. The distance between us looked life-long. I was afraid but that was okay because I'd learned something about fear. I know that the fall is fast and beyond it are shades of blue I have yet to see.

Tomorrow is a Monday.

Rachelle Robinett is a writer. She lives in New York City.